Sir Bigwart
Knight of the Wonky Table

Sir Bigwart
Knight of the
Wonky Table

Alan MacDonald

illustrations by Mark Beech

BLOOMSBURY

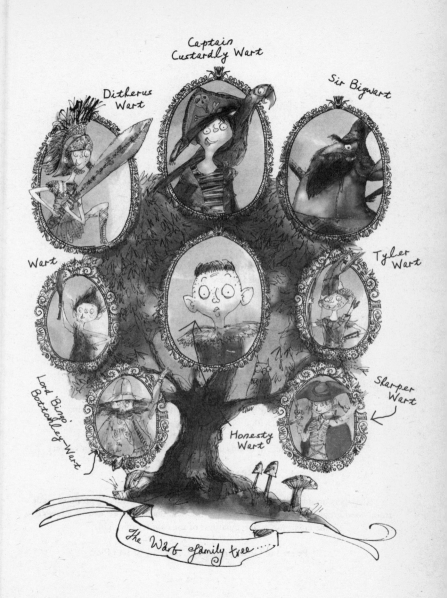

Captain
Custardly Wart

Ditherus
Wart

Sir Bigwart

Wart

Tyler
Wart

Lord 'Bunio'
Bottomley Wart

Honesty
Wart

Sharper
Wart

The Wart Family tree......

First published in Great Britain in 2008 by Bloomsbury Publishing Plc
36 Soho Square, London, W1D 3QY

A CIP catalogue record of this book is available from the British Library

ISBN 978 0 7475 9468 0

All papers used by Bloomsbury Publishing are natural, recyclable products made
from wood grown in well-managed forests. The manufacturing processes conform to
the environmental regulations of the country of origin.

Printed in Great Britain by Clays Ltd, St Ives Plc

1 3 5 7 9 10 8 6 4 2

It's Behind You!

Foreword
by
Professor Frank Lee Barking (M. A. D. Phil)

Since the dawn of time members of the hapless Wart family have been dogged by disaster. From facing flesh-eating ogres to grappling with gladiators and being kidnapped by pirates, Warts have looked Death in the eye and lived to tell the tale. Now, thanks to years of painstaking research, and literally hours of daydreaming, I am proud to bring you the absolutely true and epic saga of ...

The History of Warts

Chapter 1

Marrying Marigold

'**O**dds frogs!' exclaimed King Eggnog the Eighth. 'At this rate there won't be any princes left to marry!'

'No indeed, sire,' agreed Lord Fawnley. 'Prince Frederick wrote to cancel his visit next week. Apart from Prince Bobbins he was the last on our list.'

'Prince Bobbins? What's wrong with him?' asked the King.

'He's six months old, my lord. I'm told he dribbles.'

The King paced up and down his throne room. It was a vexing problem. Princess Marigold was his only child and he loved her dearly, but one day she would sit on the throne of Eggnog. In his view it was high time she met a handsome prince and got married – after all, she was eleven years old. (King Eggnog never considered that his daughter could look after a kingdom perfectly well by herself. A kingdom needed a king, he said, or else it would be a queendom, which didn't sound right at all.)

'Perhaps, my lord, the Princess isn't ready for marriage yet,' said Lord Fawnley.

'Poppycock!' said the King. 'A princess without a prince is like a . . . a knight without a nightie.'

'Yes, sire, but if the Princess refuses to take one?'

'A nightie? She has hundreds of them!'

'No, sire. I meant a husband.'

'Well, that is why I'm asking you, Fawnley. You are my Lord Chamberlain, you're meant to advise me. Think, man. We need a thingummywot.'

'A plan, sire?'

'That's the fellow – a plan.'

There was a long silence while Lord Fawnley gave the matter some deep thought, stroking his pointed beard. Beards were in fashion among the knights of Eggnog and Lord Fawnley kept his as neatly trimmed as a lawn. He glanced in the mirror and remembered he was meant to be thinking.

'I think I may have it, sire,' he said.

'Go on.'

'A quest.'

'Ah, a quest! Excellent! And how would that work exactly?' asked the King, who hadn't the faintest clue what Lord Fawnley was talking about.

'I believe they are very popular with knights these days, sire. Usually they involve a long and dangerous journey with some kind of deadly peril waiting at the end.'

'Such as marrying the Princess Marigold, you mean?'

'No, my lord. Such as slaying a dragon or breaking a curse – that kind of thing.'

The King frowned. 'I see, but how is that going to help Marigold?' he asked.

'I was coming to that, sire. The knight who completes this quest will prove himself the bravest in the land. What greater reward than claiming the Princess as his bride.'

'Excellent!' said King Eggnog. 'But just one thing – if there are dragons and so forth what if the brave knight comes back missing his head?'

Lord Fawnley smiled. 'That's the beauty of it, sire, we just send someone else. Don't forget you have one hundred knights. I'm sure they're only too eager to prove their worth.'

'Fawnley,' said the King, 'you are not as stupid as you look.'

The Lord Chamberlain bowed. 'You are too kind, my lord.'

'We shall proclaim the quest tonight,' said King Eggnog. 'Tell the court to gather in the Great Hall at supper. Oh, and I nearly forgot, Fawnley – the deadly peril. What's that going to be?'

Lord Fawnley smiled to himself. 'Oh, leave that to me, Highness. I think I know just the thing.'

Chapter 2

Bigwart the Brave

The knights of Eggnog did not know that one of them was about to set forth on a dangerous adventure. If they had, they might have found some excuse to stay away from court that evening. Not one of them had ever fought a fire-breathing dragon or rescued a damsel from anything more distressing than a puddle. The truth was they were a spineless bunch of cowards. Ten of them were scared of spiders, seven didn't like the dark and at least one could never get to sleep without a bedtime story. Most of the time they stayed in the castle, feasting, drinking and playing games in the Great Hall. Their favourite game was indoor jousting, which is much like outdoor jousting except that no one gets hurt. It is played by two knights who each ride piggy-back on one of their friends. The knights charge at each other, armed with mops and buckets, and usually end up in a messy heap on the floor.

The knight who invented this game was called Sir Bigwart. Sir Bigwart had round, rosy cheeks and a nose like a knobbly potato. His armour was old and so rusty at the joints that it almost matched the red of his beard. At present his helmet was out in the stables, where a hen had laid five speckled eggs inside it.

Despite his failings, Sir Bigwart had one great talent and that was boasting. Once a year, usually in the spring, Sir Bigwart would set out from the castle, telling his friends that he was setting off in search of adventure. A few days later he would return with tales of the marvels he had seen and the daring deeds he had performed. In actual fact he never went further than the village tavern, where the bravest thing he did was fall into bed and snore till noon.

That evening there was a buzz of excitement as the knights gathered in the Great Hall. Word had already gone round that the King intended to make a royal proclamation. The King's high table wasn't big enough to seat all one hundred knights so a number had to stand, which always led to pushing and squabbling and sometimes to the table's wonky leg giving way at the most embarrassing moment. (This was the reason why King Eggnog's courtiers were known far and wide as the Knights of the Wonky Table.)

When everyone was seated, a herald stepped forward and began to read the proclamation.

'His Royal Majesty King Eggnog the Eighth, Most High and Mighty Lord of the Three Kingdoms, Duke of Camembert, Earl of Dripping ...'

'Yes, yes,' said the King, waving a hand impatiently. 'We can skip the introductions and get on to the important bit.'

The herald looked peeved and began again. 'His Royal Majesty King Eggnog the Eighth and so on and so on ... proclaims a quest. Whosoever shall complete this quest may claim the hand of Her Royal Highness Princess Marigold in marriage.'

Princess Marigold jumped to her feet, her eyes blazing. 'WHAT?' she thundered.

'Oh Marigold, my sweet, I didn't see you there,' said the King.

'You're going to *give me away*?' fumed the Princess. 'Make me the prize in one of your stupid games?'

'Well, no, my buttercup, it's not a game, it's called a quest . . .' stammered the King.

The Princess picked up a bowl of venison soup and drew back her arm.

'I don't care what it's called!' she shrieked. 'If you think I'm marrying one of your pea-brained knights, you can think again!'

CRASH! The plate narrowly missed the King's head, splattering the wall with brown soup.

'Now, now, my pigeon,' said the King, ducking below the table. 'Can't we talk sensibly about this?'

Smash! A bowl of elderflower jelly hit the wall, followed by a mutton pasty.

'Help!' cried the King. 'Guards!'

Two of the palace guards stepped forward and seized the Princess by the arms. She was dragged

protesting from the room before anything else got broken (the King's nose, for example).

'Thank goodness!' sighed the King. 'Now, where were we?'

'You were offering the Princess's hand, my lord,' prompted Lord Fawnley.

'Ah yes,' said the King. 'And remind me, what is this quest going to be exactly?'

Lord Fawnley stood up and waited for silence. 'The knight who wishes to win the hand of Princess Marigold,' he said, 'must slay the Ogres of Ghastly Fell.'

A deathly silence fell over the room, broken only by a dull *clunk!* as the wonky table leg gave way and one hundred bowls of soup slid to one end. The knights sank lower in their chairs. None of them had ever set eyes on an ogre and they wanted to keep it that way. Ogres were like giants only much much worse. If you were lucky you might run into a good-natured giant on your travels, but friendly ogres did not exist. Ogres were bone-crunching brutes who ate knights for breakfast. And of all the ogres in the land none were as fearsome as the Ogres of Ghastly Fell. These ogres were twin brothers, which meant they were double the trouble – and probably triple the smell.

King Eggnog smiled pleasantly. 'So. Which of you brave knights wishes to take up the challenge? Step forward – don't be shy.'

The knights of Eggnog stared at the table and fiddled with their napkins.

'Come, Sir Horace. What about you?' asked the King.

'Nothing would give me greater pleasure, my lord,'

blustered Sir Horace, 'but my sword is at the blacksmith's and won't be back till the end of the month.'

'Sir Runcible, what about you?' asked the King.

'Alas, my horse stumbled in a ditch yesterday, my lord. It has gone lame.'

'What rotten luck!' said the King. 'But Sir Cardigan, surely you will go?'

Sir Cardigan pulled out a hanky and blew his nose. 'I would, by lord, but I hab the most tebbible cold.'

'Oh, this is ridiculous!' said King Eggnog. 'You are meant to be the bravest and boldest knights in the land. Surely one of you will go?'

Lord Fawnley had noticed one of the knights had left the table and was trying to sneak out of the room on all fours.

'Sir Bigwart!' he called out. 'What about you?'

'Me?' said Sir Bigwart, raising his head as everyone turned in his direction.

'Yes,' said Lord Fawnley. 'Remember that giant you fought only last year? You told us all about it.'

'Ah yes,' said Sir Bigwart, getting to his feet sheepishly. 'But he was only a small giant – not much bigger than an oak tree really.'

'Come now, Bigwart, don't be so modest,' smiled

12

Sir Horace. 'I remember you telling me you've always wanted to meet an ogre face to face.'

'Er . . . did I?' mumbled Sir Bigwart.

'Yes! You said if you ever met one, you'd slice him into sausage meat.'

The other knights around the table murmured in agreement. They had all heard Sir Bigwart making boasts of this kind.

'Well, of course,' said Sir Bigwart, 'slaying an ogre or two would usually be no trouble at all for a knight like myself, but –'

'Excellent!' interrupted King Eggnog. 'Then that's settled. Go home and pack what you need for the journey. We will all be there to see you off in the morning. And remember, when you come back triumphant, Princess Marigold will be waiting for you.'

'Oh, ah . . . thank you, sire,' said Sir Bigwart feebly.

He couldn't decide which was worse: facing a pair of flesh-eating, blood-dripping ogres or Princess Marigold in a temper.

Chapter 3
Knight of the Bedchamber

S ir Bigwart lived in a large, draughty manor house with his mother. The next morning Lady Alice searched everywhere for him and eventually she found him hiding under a bed.

'There you are, Biggy!' she exclaimed. 'What on earth are you doing?'

'Shhh!' replied the brave knight. 'I'm not here!'

'Well, of course you are, you big lump! I can see you. Come out!'

'I can't, Mother! If anyone knocks on the door, you don't know where I am.'

'You're under the bed!'

'No I'm not!'

'You are! I can see your bottom sticking out.'

Sir Bigwart made an effort to pull in his bottom but there wasn't much room under the bed for a knight of his proportions so he only succeeded in bumping his head.

'Ow!' he hissed. 'Go *away*, Mother! I'm trying to hide.'

'Hide? From who?'

'From the King. From everyone. They want me to go on a horrible quest.'

'Well, I know, dumpling – everyone at court's talking about it,' said Lady Alice. 'I'm coming to the castle gates to wave you off.'

Sir Bigwart sighed heavily. 'Mother, I'm not going! It's certain death. They want me to slay the Ogres of Fell.'

'Goodness!' tutted Lady Alice. 'What a fuss over a silly old ogre!'

'Two silly old ogres if you don't mind,' objected Sir Bigwart huffily.

15

'What's the difference? They're only ogres! Are you coming out or not?'

'Not,' said Sir Bigwart stubbornly.

'Please yourself,' said Lady Alice. 'Then I suppose you won't be wanting any breakfast?' Lady Alice knew her son well and if there was one word that could tempt him out from under a bed it was the word breakfast. (The words lunch, supper and elevenses had a similar effect.)

'What sort of breakfast?' he asked.

'Honey cakes. Your favourite.'

'I'm not hungry,' replied the knight.

'Good. All the more for me then.'

Soon after there was a knock on the door and a kitchen boy entered, bringing a plate piled high with honey cakes, fresh out of the oven. The boy's name was Crispin. He was a cheerful boy with a round, innocent face and a haircut that resembled an upside-down pudding bowl. He had baked the honey cakes himself. (He did almost everything in the kitchen since the cook was extremely short-sighted. She had once put the cat in the oven, mistaking it for a plucked chicken.)

Under the bed, Sir Bigwart could hear his mother munching away and giving little sighs of pleasure. There is nothing worse, he thought, than listening to someone slurping honey cakes when you are starving hungry.

'How are they?' he asked.

'Delicious. Light as a feather,' said Lady Alice. A crumb dropped on the floor. A hand sneaked out from under the bed and the crumb vanished. A

moment later Sir Bigwart's head appeared, followed by the rest of his body.

'So,' said Lady Alice, when they had both sat down. 'When do you set off?'

Her son looked miserable. 'I'm not going anywhere. They want me to slay an ogre, Mother. Two ogres. I could quite possibly die.'

'Don't be such a big softie,' said his mother. 'What about that seven-headed dragon you killed?'

'Ogres are different,' grumbled Sir Bigwart.

'Nonsense! Have you ever seen one? People think ogres are huge, horrible blood-sucking brutes, but they might be harmless as kittens. How many people do you know who have actually met an ogre in the flesh?'

'None,' said Sir Bigwart gloomily. 'They're probably all dead.'

'Look on the bright side,' said Lady Alice, taking another honey cake. 'If you succeed, you'll be famous.'

'Will I?'

'Of course! The King will throw a banquet in your honour and I'll be able to buy a new hat.'

'A hat? What on earth for?'

'For your wedding, silly – to Princess Marigold.'

'Oh, that!' groaned Sir Bigwart.

'Have you thought what it would mean – marrying a princess?'

'Yes. I'd never get any peace.'

'It would mean you wouldn't be a common knight any more, you'd be a prince. Prince Bigwart. How does that sound?'

Sir Bigwart liked the sound of it. If he was a prince, he would have his own royal coat of arms and an army of servants to wait on him hand and foot. All the other knights would have to stand up when he entered a room. Instead of 'Warty' and 'Bignose' they'd have to call him 'sire' and 'my lord'. Even that fathead Lord Fawnley. Maybe his mother was right. A quest wasn't such a bad idea. After all, he didn't have to actually fight any ogres – he could just ride around looking for them (or, better, still *pretending* to look for them). There was only one drawback – Ghastly Fell lay to the north of the kingdom. That meant crossing the Whispering Wood and he didn't fancy going there by himself either.

'It's no good,' he said. 'I don't have a squire. Knights never set off on a quest without a squire.'

'But Biggy, darling, where are we going to find a squire before tomorrow?' asked Lady Alice.

Sir Bigwart helped himself to the last of the cakes. Eating helped him think. Where could they find a suitable squire? Someone brave, loyal and good at handing you things – like honey cakes, for instance. At that moment there was a knock on the door and Crispin returned.

Lady Alice clapped her hands. 'Of course! Crispin! He can be your squire!'

'Crispin?' said Sir Bigwart. 'But he's the kitchen boy! I can't take him!'

Crispin looked disappointed. It was true he didn't look much like a squire. He was dressed in a mud-brown tunic and a filthy apron stained with eggs, flour and gravy. His hair – as we've already mentioned

– looked like it had been cut by a mad butcher.

'Never mind that,' said Lady Alice. 'A bath and a new set of clothes – we'll soon smarten him up. Crispin, how would you like to accompany your master on an exciting adventure?'

'Very much, my lady,' answered Crispin.

'Humph!' grunted Sir Bigwart. 'Come here, boy. What do you know about being a squire?'

'I know how to do what I'm told,' answered Crispin.

'Quite right,' said Sir Bigwart. 'But the life of a knight can be hard. There will be daring and danger and whatnot. Are you steadfast and brave?'

'I'm not frightened of rats,' replied Crispin.

'Well, it's a start, I suppose,' grunted Sir Bigwart. 'What about ogres?'

'I think I might be a little scared if I met an ogre,' said Crispin truthfully. 'Especially if he was tall as a mountain and wanted to eat me. But I wouldn't run away.'

'Really? You wouldn't?'

'No, I'd ask him if he liked honey cakes,' said Crispin. 'My honey cakes are the best in the kingdom.'

Sir Bigwart doubted that this would cut much ice with an ogre. Generally ogres are more interested in biting off your head or one of your legs – they have little time for honey cakes. All the same, he thought, it couldn't hurt to have a squire who knew something about cooking. They had a long journey ahead of them and a knight couldn't live on fresh air.

Thus it was that the matter was settled and Crispin became Sir Bigwart's new squire. He went off to hunt for his master's rusty armour. But first he had to do something that would test his courage to the limit – he had to take a bath.

Chapter 4

The Runaway Princess

K ing Eggnog knocked softly on his daughter's
bedroom door.

'Marigold, my sweet? Are you there?'

'GO AWAY!' yelled the Princess, who didn't sound
in a very good mood.

'Sugarplum! It's me, Daddy. Open the door.'

'I'm not speaking to you!' There was a brief silence.
'Well, I am only speaking to you to tell you that I'm
not speaking to you.'

'It's time to go. Everyone's waiting. Don't you want to come and wave them off?' asked the King.

There was no answer. The Princess wasn't speaking to him. This happened quite a lot. Sometimes she didn't speak to him for a whole minute. King Eggnog tried again.

'Poppet? Surely you're not still cross about last night?'

The door flew open and Marigold stood there with a silver hairbrush. The King stepped back – in the Princess's hand a hairbrush was a deadly weapon.

'You really expect me to agree to this?' she stormed.

'I only want you to come downstairs.'

'I mean to marrying this . . . this Bigwig nitwit.'

'Oh. Sir Bigwart.'

'I've seen him! He's old and ugly and he has a horrible beard. And he's vain and boastful and fat and ugly.'

'He can't be ugly twice,' the King pointed out.

'He's not even a prince, he's a common knight!' The Princess was brushing her golden hair so violently that the King thought she might set it on fire.

'But, sugarplum,' he said, 'you didn't like any of the

princes you met. You pushed Prince Dudley down the stairs.'

'He tried to kiss my hand,' said Marigold.

'This will be different,' said the King. 'This way you'll be marrying a brave and handsome knight. Brave anyway. Someone who has killed an ogre to prove his worth. Two ogres actually.'

The Princess stamped her foot. It was only a dainty foot but when she stamped it people jumped and servants ran for cover. 'I've told you,' she said. 'I am not marrying this Bogwart. Not if he brings back a dragon with a ring through its nose.'

King Eggnog looked alarmed. He hoped Sir Bigwart wouldn't be bringing home any dragons.

'The thing is, my sweet, it's a matter of honour. I've given my word that you'll marry whoever completes the quest. And a king's word is his, you know ... his word. You'll see – it will all work out for the best. Every princess wants to get married and live happily ever after.'

'I do not,' said Marigold. 'And if you try to make me, I shall ... I shall run away!'

'And where would you run to, my buttercup?' chuckled the King. 'Why don't you go and put on your pretty blue gown and come downstairs with me? There's a gallant knight outside who's very –'

THUD! The Princess had slammed the door. King Eggnog shook his head and went downstairs.

Left alone, Princess Marigold flopped down in the window seat and looked out over the courtyard. It seemed as if half the village had gathered to cheer Sir Bigwart on his way. She could see him riding his horse through the crowd, waving his sword as if he'd already won a great battle. He certainly wasn't

a princess's dream. The plume of his helmet drooped like a limp daffodil and his armour was so rusty it looked like it might fall apart. Beside him his squire trudged along, loaded down with hams, honey cakes and other essentials for a knight going on a dangerous journey.

The crowd cheered as Sir Bigwart turned his horse towards the gates. How wonderful, thought Marigold, to be setting off on an adventure, not knowing what tomorrow would bring! Marigold always knew what tomorrow would bring. Her father was always saying she should behave more like a princess. In practice this meant lolling around reading poetry or wandering the palace gardens or listening to dull princes who were as vain as peacocks. The sad truth was the Princess didn't have any friends of her own age and she'd certainly never had anything like an adventure.

She suddenly noticed how quiet the palace had become. It sounded as if everyone had gone to the gates to wave Sir Bigwart off. Pushing open the door, she saw there was no guard at the top of the stairs. A daring idea came to her.

* * *

Once they were out of sight of the palace walls, Sir Bigwart pulled on his reins. All that waving to admirers had made him peckish. He announced that they would stop for a rest and a morsel to eat. Crispin looked surprised.

'But my lord,' he said, 'we haven't come half a mile. Shouldn't we push on through the forest?'

His master's reply was drowned out by a loud drumming of hoofs. Thundering towards them at high speed was a white horse with a knight seated on its back. Actually, 'seated' wasn't really the word – the knight looked like he was clinging on for dear life. His arms were wrapped round the horse's neck while the rest of him was slipping out of the saddle.

'Heeeeeeeeeeeeeeeeelp!' he screamed, galloping past at tremendous speed. Sir Bigwart wiped a speck of mud from his eye.

'What did he say?'

'I think he said: "Heeeeeeeeeeeeeelp!" sire,' replied Crispin.

'That's what I thought,' said Sir Bigwart. A startled yell reached them. The white horse had suddenly pulled up, catapulting its rider over its head. Luckily

the knight landed in something soft – a large muddy puddle.

Crispin ran over to help. The horse had galloped off, leaving the knight sitting in the puddle having a tantrum. He was wearing a red velvet robe. Below this peeped white petticoats and a pair of dainty silver slippers When he pulled off his helmet, out tumbled a long coil of golden hair. Crispin thought he was looking at an angel.

'Well, don't just stand there, stupid! Help me up!' stormed Princess Marigold.

Crispin flushed a deep pink. Ever since last summer, when he'd caught sight of the Princess wandering in the palace gardens, he had fallen hopelessly in love. Normally it is pointless for a kitchen boy to love a princess – princesses sleep in palaces while kitchen boys sleep with the dogs. But Crispin believed that if he could only meet his golden angel and speak to her something magical would happen. So when Princess Marigold held out a muddy hand to him it was the moment he'd dreamed of a thousand times. That was why he went very pink and mumbled something like 'Oh, um, sorry . . .' and then bowed so low he almost fell over. Princess Marigold rolled her eyes and squelched past him, muttering to herself.

'Look at me! I'm filthy!'

'You are, um, well, a bit muddy,' said Crispin, wishing he could think of something witty and clever to say.

'Well, don't stand there mumbling, do something! Fetch me some clean clothes!'

Crispin looked around as if he thought a silk dress might be growing on one of the nearby trees. Sir Bigwart arrived on Hotspur and climbed down off his horse.

'Princess Marigold!' he exclaimed.

'Oh. You're Sir Bigwit.'

'Wart.'

'What?'

'No, Wart. Sir Bigwart. I am Sir Bigwart.'

'You don't have to keep repeating it – I'm not deaf,' said the Princess.

'How may I be of service?' asked the knight, making a stiff bow, which was the best he could manage in a rusty suit of armour. 'Are you lost? Shall I have my squire escort you back to the palace?'

'Lost?' snorted the Princess. 'Of course I'm not lost. I've run away from home. I'd have thought even an idiot could see that.'

'Oh,' said Sir Bigwart. It explained why the Princess was dressed in men's clothes. 'And where were you running to?' he asked.

'Are you always this slow?' she snapped, rolling her eyes. 'I'm coming with you!'

'With me?'

'Yes! You've no idea how boring it is being a princess – everyone telling you what to do all the time. That's why I decided it's high time I had an adventure.'

Sir Bigwart was looking flustered. He wasn't used to dealing with runaway princesses.

'I am sorry, Highness,' he said, 'but it's out of the question. We can't possibly take you along.'

The Princess's eyes flashed dangerously. Her cheeks had turned red – a sure sign that she was about to explode.

'You dare to say "No" to me?'

'Your Highness,' sighed Sir Bigwart, 'it's not that I don't want your company – nothing would give me greater pleasure, but a quest is no place for a princess.

There may be daring and danger ahead of us. Wolves in the forest and hobgoblins in the trees.'

'And ogres – don't forget the ogres,' added Crispin.

The Princess stamped her foot, splattering them all with mud. 'If you don't take me with you, I shall scream,' she warned.

Sir Bigwart laughed softly. 'Do as you like, Highness. My advice is to go back to the palace and change out of those wet clothes before you catch a chill.'

He swung himself back into the saddle and plodded off on Hotspur. Crispin followed behind, glancing back over his shoulder at the furious princess. They hadn't gone twenty paces when an ear-splitting scream stopped them in their tracks.

'HEEEELP! THIEVES! MURDERERS!'

When Princess Marigold screamed, rabbits ran for cover, crows flew startled from the treetops and Hotspur reared up, almost throwing his master from the saddle. Sir Bigwart pulled on the reins and turned back. If anyone heard the Princess shrieking like that, they were all in trouble. The King would probably chop off their heads.

'HEEEEELLP!'

34

'All right! Stop, stop!' pleaded Sir Bigwart.

The Princess stopped in mid-scream and smiled at them sweetly. 'Then I can come?'

'Yes, yes,' sighed Sir Bigwart. 'As long as you promise never to do that again.'

The Princess reached up a hand. 'Good. Then help me up.'

'What?'

'I'm a princess. You don't expect me to walk? Since my horse has run off I'll have to ride behind you. Boy, kneel down.'

Poor Crispin knelt down on all fours in the mud while the Princess used him as a mounting block to climb up on to Hotspur's back. Sir Bigwart shook his head. They hadn't got half a mile from home and already this quest was turning into a disaster. The last thing he needed was to babysit a spoilt princess.

Trotting along beside them, Crispin hummed a tune to himself. In his view, life could hardly get much better. Yesterday he was a humble kitchen boy dressed in rags. Today he was a squire setting off in search of adventure and the most beautiful princess in the world had actually spoken to him (even if it was to call him 'stupid'). *Who knows?* thought Crispin. In a few days' time I might even be able to speak to her without blushing.

Chapter 5

Whispering Wood

Night was falling as the three of them journeyed on through Whispering Wood. Princess Marigold shivered with cold. She wasn't used to being out in the woods after dark. Crispin kept a tight hold on Hotspur's bridle in case he got left behind. They had been travelling all day and now they were hungry, tired and aching.

'Are we almost there?' asked Marigold.

'Not far now,' replied Sir Bigwart.

'You said that an hour ago. Are you sure you know where we are?'

Sir Bigwart knew exactly where they were. They were lost. It seemed to him they had been travelling through the same part of the forest all day. In the darkness, the trees all looked much the same, apart from the ones that looked like witches and hobgoblins. The wind stirred the branches above his head and the brave knight clutched at his sword.

'You're not scared, are you?' asked Princess Marigold.

'Scared? Me?' scoffed Sir Bigwart. 'I am a knight of Eggnog!'

'Only, your armour keeps squeaking.'

'It does that when it's cold,' said Sir Bigwart. 'Anyway, it's not the first time I've been lost in a forest.'

'I thought you said we *weren't* lost,' frowned the Princess.

'We're not. We're just not where I thought we were.'

'Sire,' interrupted Crispin, 'I may be wrong but haven't we crossed this stream before?'

Sir Bigwart didn't know. Streams were like trees – they all looked the same in the dark. What he needed was a big broad path, preferably with a large arrow pointing ahead saying 'This Way out of the Forest'. He was beginning to regret coming on this quest. Whatever possessed him to think he could fight a pair of ogres? All day long Marigold had done nothing but grumble. Her clothes were wet through, her slippers were muddy and her feet were cold. She seemed to believe there was a palace around every corner where you could find a bed for the night and servants to run you a warm bath. If he ever got out of this forest, he vowed he would never boast about anything again.

Crispin pulled on Hotspur's bridle and stopped to sniff the air.

'Sire, I can smell something.'

'It's not my fault,' replied Sir Bigwart. 'Armour makes me sweat.'

'No, not that. I think I can smell woodsmoke.'

Sir Bigwart sniffed. 'Well, what of it?'

'Sire,' said Crispin, 'if there is smoke then it's coming from a fire. And if there's a fire then perhaps there's a house! And if there's a house –'

'Yes, yes, I get the point,' said Sir Bigwart.

Crispin was right. Following the stream, they

eventually came to a small stone cottage beside a wooden bridge. Smoke curled from the chimney and the windows glowed with warm light. Crispin had never seen a more welcoming sight in all his life.

Sir Bigwart rapped on the door but it creaked open by itself. Inside, the cottage was cramped, dark and untidy. An ancient black pot bubbled over a fire, filling the room with the smell of woodsmoke. Crispin peered inside but could see nothing but clouds of smoke that rose up the chimney.

In every corner there were stacks of dusty leather-bound books rising almost as high as the beams of the roof. Books crammed the shelves on the walls and lay open on the table. Crispin picked up the top book and read the title: *Talking to Toads*. Underneath he found *101 Easy Curses* and *The Wizard Book of Spells (Volume 3 1/2)*. He had an uneasy sense they were being watched. Looking up, he saw a snowy owl staring down on him from the rafters with large amber eyes.

'Sire,' he whispered, 'I'm not sure this is safe. There's something odd about this place.'

'What's odd about it?' asked Sir Bigwart. 'It's

warm and dry and out of the wind. What could be better?' He pushed a pile of books on to the floor and flopped down in a chair with a weary sigh. Crispin knelt at his feet and began the struggle to pull off his rusty armour.

Princess Marigold cleared her throat loudly. 'And who is going to show me to my room?'

Crispin looked around. She seemed to be under the impression that there was a secret staircase leading to the upper rooms.

'Um, I think this is the only room there is, Highness,' said Crispin.

'Don't be ridiculous! There must be bedrooms. Where am I supposed to sleep?'

'Try the floor,' yawned Sir Bigwart, who had already bagged the only armchair for himself.

Princess Marigold looked at the floor. It was bare and filthy. There were probably spiders lurking in the corners. She shivered.

'Very well,' she said. 'Boy, bring the sheets and pillows and make up the bed.'

Crispin looked at Sir Bigwart, who just rolled his eyes.

'Which sheets and pillows?' asked Crispin.

'The ones you brought with you, of course!'

At a loss, Crispin took off his own cloak and folded it several times before handing it to Marigold.

'What is this?'

'My cloak, Highness. You can use it as a blanket to keep you warm.'

Marigold wrinkled her nose as if she might catch something nasty. She made a feeble attempt at moving piles of dusty books to clear a space.

'Well?' she said, looking at them pointedly.

'What now?' groaned Sir Bigwart.

'You may leave me while I get ready for bed.'

Outside it had started to rain. Crispin and his master shivered while they waited for permission to go back in.

'Princesses!' snorted Sir Bigwart. 'They're nothing but trouble.'

'Are they?' asked Crispin. 'I suppose you've met quite a few?'

'Hundreds.'

'How do you . . . I mean, what do you say to them?' asked Crispin. 'When I'm with the Princess my words all get muddled.'

'I wouldn't bother!' grunted Sir Bigwart. 'They don't want to talk about anything interesting like horses or hunting. Princesses only want to talk about themselves.'

'Do they?'

'Oh yes. They want you to admire their eyes, their teeth, and so on.'

This was news to Crispin. 'What about their teeth exactly?' he said.

'Oh, you know – they're bright as the moon, they

shine like the stars – that sort of drivel. If you really want to impress a princess, write her a poem. Poetry never fails.'

'Really?'

'Take it from me. Read them a poem and they practically fall into a swoon.'

Crispin was greatly cheered by this (though it didn't occur to him that Sir Bigwart might not be the best person to ask). As it happened, Crispin had already written a number of poems about Princess Marigold. He made them up when he was chopping onions in the kitchen (onions always put him in the right mood). Perhaps, if he could pluck up the courage, he could recite one of his poems to Marigold.

The rain was falling steadily.

'Come on,' said Sir Bigwart. 'Let's go in before I rust away.'

Back inside, the Princess had blown out the candle on the table and was tucked up under Crispin's cloak. Her red robe hung from a bookshelf to dry. Crispin helped his master out of his armour and left him curled up in the armchair to sleep. He could see Marigold's hair tumbling loose over her pillow. Hidden in the darkness, he didn't feel quite so shy.

'Marigold!' he whispered, creeping closer. 'Marigold?'

The Princess mumbled something he didn't catch.

'It's me. Crispin. I wondered if I could . . . well . . . read you one of my poems.'

No answer. He wasn't sure if Marigold was actually awake.

'It's not very long. Actually, it's only one verse.'

Silence again. Having got this far, Crispin decided it was now or never. He took a deep breath and began.

> *'Ogres are big,*
> *Giants are tall,*
> *Witches are ugly*
> *But you're not at all.'*

He waited for Marigold to swoon or sigh or at least turn her head and look at him, but she did none of these things. She had probably slept through the whole thing. Disappointed, he rose to his feet and turned away.

'Crispin?'

45

'Yes?'

'Get some sleep,' said Marigold.

'Oh. Right. Good idea,' replied Crispin. He crept away on tiptoe, feeling utterly ridiculous.

If the darkness hadn't hidden Marigold's face, he would have seen she was smiling.

Sir Bigwart was dreaming. In his dream he was battling heroically against a giant blackberry pie. The pie was growing bigger all the time and the only solution was for someone to eat it. Sir Bigwart's sword sliced open the brown crust and blackberries oozed out. His enemy was making small, snuffling noises which seemed out of character for a fruit pie.

His eyes blinked open. Two small black eyes stared

back at him from either side of a bristly snout. For a moment he thought he was still dreaming, but he could feel warm breath on his face. The animal staring at him was covered in coarse, dark hair and had two savage-looking tusks. Suddenly it came to him: it was a boar – a wild boar – and it was deciding whether to eat him.

'YAAAARGH!' Sir Bigwart shot out of his chair as if he'd been stung by a hornet. The wild boar toppled backwards with a surprised squeal. It scrambled to its feet and gave him an offended look. Sir Bigwart seized the nearest weapon to hand, which happened to be one of his gauntlets. It wasn't much use but at least he could poke it in the eye.

Crispin and Marigold had woken up and were both staring at the boar in amazement, partly because it was wearing a bottle-green velvet cloak tied round its neck. Waking up in the morning to find a wild boar on top of you is surprising enough, but what happened next was an even greater shock. The boar opened its mouth and spoke.

'You'll have to forgive the mess,' it said. 'I wasn't expecting visitors.'

Chapter 6

An Odour of Ogres

Meanwhile, a few miles north, a castle was stirring into life ...

It was built of grey stone which over the years had cracked and crumbled away. Parts of it had fallen into the green, foul-smelling slime that was the moat. Moss grew in the castle's damp courtyards and ivy invaded the walls. The battlements looked out over Ghastly Fell where, even in spring, the fog was so thick that nothing could be seen but the ghostly shapes of trees. It was a place where the sun never shone and the birds never sang. People said that if anyone went into the castle, they never came out.

Right now thumps and bumps could be heard upstairs. It was just after noon and the ogres had risen from their beds. You might think that twin ogres would be fond of each other, but you'd be mistaken. Dungbean and Grimbeard could never be in the same room without squabbling and fighting. Sometimes they argued for hours, even for days at a time, roaring and stamping their giant feet so that anyone listening would imagine it was an earthquake. When they weren't squabbling or sleeping, they were thinking about food. Ogres are not vegetarians – their favourite meal is red meat. Best of all, they like human flesh. Raw, roast, fried or boiled – it doesn't matter to an ogre.

Grimbeard yawned and scratched his hairy armpit as he thumped downstairs. He was as ugly an ogre as you could wish to meet. His hair was matted and filthy while his beard was so gigantic it covered his mountainous belly. A beard as thick as a hedge can be useful and Grimbeard's wasn't just for show. Sometimes he would reach into it and pull out a titbit he'd been saving since breakfast. Over time his beard had become speckled and crusty with bread-crumbs, egg, bacon and jam, but Grimbeard didn't notice – he still imagined he was as dazzling as a prince and certainly much better looking than his grisly brother.

'So is I!' replied his twin. 'My bellies has been gurgling like a drainpipe ever since I got up!'

'Then why didn't you set the trap last night like I is telling you?' demanded Grimbeard.

'What is you drivelling about? I did!'

'*Did?* You never did!'

'I is telling you, muckslop! Last night I was out there setting it.'

'The trap?'

'Are you dim as a dunghill? What is I just saying to you?'

This went on for some time since the ogres could turn the simplest conversation into a furious argument. They clenched their fists and furrowed their brows, trying to think of worse insults to call each other. Finally they remembered that they were hungry and there was no chance of any breakfast until they checked to see if they had caught anything in their traps.

The trap Dungbean had set was a simple one. (Ogres may be big but they are not famous for their intelligence.) It was a deep muddy hole in the ground and if anything fell into the hole it was trapped (as simple as that). You might think that a whopping great hole would be obvious to anyone, but the giants set their trap by covering it each night with Grimbeard's hanky and a scattering of leaves. In any case, Ghastly Fell was so foggy that most days it was hard to see your nose in front of your face. Even the ogres had stepped in their own trap on many occasions. But today their luck was in. When Grimbeard peered into the trap, he saw two large brown eyes gazing up at him.

''Tis a milkmulcher!' he said. The cow rolled its head and mooed pitifully.

'Well, what is you waiting for? Pull it out!' urged Dungbean.

Grimbeard got down on his knees and reached into the hole. The poor beast swung round dizzily as it was lifted into the air.

''Tis not much of a breakfast,' grumbled Dungbean. 'One swallop and it will be gone.'

''Tain't enough for the both of us,' agreed Grimbeard with a sly grin. 'And as I catched it I should be the one to scoffle it.'

'YOU, gobfungus?' roared Dungbean. 'I is the one that set the trap.'

'But I is the one that told you to do it!'

'Give it to me, duncebungler!' growled Dungbean, trying to grab the cow.

'Not on your bellies, hogbreath!'

Dungbean grabbed his brother by the beard. Grimbeard yelled and seized his twin by the hair. The ogres bellowed and struggled and grunted as they rolled over and over. Grimbeard forgot about the cow and dropped it. Scrambling to its feet, it trotted off looking rather dazed. It might have escaped if Dungbean hadn't spotted it first.

'Look! The squizzler is getting away!' he roared.

Dungbean raised one of his feet and brought it down with a horrible squelch.

He bent down to look. ''Tis a bit flattened,' he said. 'It looks like a pancake.'

But his twin brother wasn't listening. Grimbeard had got to his feet and was sniffing the air like a hound catching a scent.

'Listen, I smells something,' he leered with a horrible grin.

'What?'

'Whomans,' replied Grimbeard.

Dungbean's eyes lit up, the fight instantly forgotten. 'Where?' he asked.

'Not far,' said Grimbeard. 'Set the trap, bimstinkle. Tonight we will catch us a supper worth the scoffling.'

Chapter 7

The Wizard Firkin

Back at the cottage, Sir Bigwart was staring open-mouthed at the wild boar.

'Did I dream it or did it just speak?' he asked.

'Of course I spoke,' replied the wild boar. It hopped on to the chair, blinking its small black eyes. 'I suppose I must look a bit strange, but then I wasn't expecting to come home and find you sleeping in my house.'

'*Your* house? I thought hogs lived in the forest,' said Princess Marigold.

'I wish you wouldn't keep calling me a hog,' said the wild boar peevishly. 'My name is Firkin. The wizard Firkin.' He attempted a dignified bow but since he was sitting on his velvet cloak he almost succeeded in throttling himself.

'If you're a wizard, why do you look like a pig?' asked Marigold.

'Ah,' said Firkin. 'That was an accident. I'm not actually qualified as a wizard, you see. I'm still what

he had somehow read the wrong page in his book of magic. The next thing he knew, he had grown four legs and a tail and was snuffling around on the floor.

'But if you're a wizard, why can't you undo the spell?' asked Crispin.

'Alas,' said Firkin, 'I wish it was that simple, but as I said, I'm only an apprentice and I need help to break the spell. I went to my master's house but he's gone to visit the Wizard Mandrake and I've no idea when he'll be back. Till then I'm stuck like this.'

Firkin sat down among his piles of books looking extremely sorry for himself.

Sir Bigwart reached for his helmet. 'Well, I wish we could help but we really ought to be going.'

'We can't just leave him!' protested Crispin. 'Didn't you say you can't break the spell on your own?'

on himself when he had...

ing he had been practising a harmless sneezing spell
studying for his Advanced Spelling Test. That morn-
table. He lived alone in the wood where he was
ing every now and then to rub himself against the
He went on to explain what had...

do wha...

'Oh, wit...

any enchantment.'

'NO,' said Marigold flatly. 'I can...

'It's only one little kiss,' said Crispin. 'It's the least we can do.'

'WE?' cried Marigold. 'Nobody's asking you to kiss a smelly old pig.'

'Please,' begged Firkin. 'I'd be very grateful. And if you'd rather close your eyes, I promise I won't be offended.' He hopped up on to the chair and presented his snout to be kissed. The Princess groaned.

Sir Bigwart and Crispin were trying not to laugh.

'Swear you will never repeat this to anyone,' said the Princess.

'I promise,' said Crispin.

'Pig's honour,' nodded Sir Bigwart.

Marigold approached the boar waiting patiently on the chair. She leaned forward slowly with her eyes screwed shut until her lips brushed something warm and damp. It was Firkin's snout. The next moment there was a flash of bright light and, instead of the boar, a young man with wild black hair sat there looking rather dazed.

Marigold jumped back and wiped her lips with the back of her hand.

'Ugh!' she said. 'I am never doing that again.'

Firkin inspected his hands and felt his nose to see if it was a snout. 'It worked!' he cried. 'I'm back! Thank you, thank you, dear Princess!' He threw his arms around Marigold and would have kissed her again if she hadn't shoved him away from her.

'I'm sorry,' he said, 'but you've no idea what a relief it is to be back to my old self. Tell me, is there anything I can do for you in return?'

'Well,' said Sir Bigwart, 'we haven't had any breakfast.'

Crispin had forgotten how hungry he was. None of them had eaten anything since yesterday afternoon when they'd finished the last of the honey cakes. But looking round, he couldn't see what Firkin was planning to cook them. There was nothing in the house except piles of old books.

'Princess,' said Firkin, 'what would you like? Name it – anything at all.'

'Can you make porridge?' asked Marigold. 'Warm porridge with cream and nutmeg?'

Firkin bowed. 'Nothing could be easier.'

'Oh – and ham. With eggs if you happen to have some.'

'Porridge, ham and eggs? Will that be all?' smiled Firkin.

'Quite all,' said Marigold. 'I'm not that hungry.'

Firkin turned to the large black iron pot, which was bubbling quietly to itself even though the fire had burned out. 'Please stand well back,' he warned. 'Never get too close when magic is at work.'

He stretched out his arms, spreading his cloak like a peacock's feathers, and spoke in a loud voice.

'Cooking pot, cooking pot,
Hear my request,
Ham, eggs and porridge
And only the best!'

No sooner had he finished speaking, than the black pot began to bubble and boil. Thick clouds of smoke rose from within, turning first blue then green then violet before their eyes. Finally the pot gave a great belch and something flew out. Firkin caught it neatly in his hands. It was a large bowl filled with steaming

porridge and topped with a thick slice of ham and three poached eggs.

'Ah,' said Firkin. 'Perhaps I should have ordered the porridge first.'

Sir Bigwart stared at the food in amazement. 'By the stars!' he said. 'How did you do that?'

'Magic,' said Firkin, with a wave of his hand. 'I told you I'm a wizard. The pot can cook you anything you desire. All you have to do is ask.'

The warm porridge filled their empty stomachs and no one left a scrap in the bowl. When they had all finished, Sir Bigwart rose to his feet and thanked their host and said they must be on their way.

'We've a long way to go if we're to reach the Castle of Fell,' he said.

Firkin gave him a strange look. 'The ogres' castle?'

'Yes. You've heard of it?'

'Heard of it? It's a few miles to the north – through the forest and across the moor. But why would anyone want to go there?'

'We are on a quest,' said Crispin. 'My master has sworn to kill the ogres.'

Sir Bigwart coughed. 'I wouldn't say sworn exactly. And in any case, we're not in any great hurry.'

'Nonsense!' said Marigold. 'The sooner you slay these horrible ogres the sooner we can all go home!'

'I must say I admire your courage,' said Firkin. 'Most people are terrified of ogres.'

'Oh, an ogre or two is nothing to me,' boasted Sir Bigwart. 'I've fought giants ten times as big and killed them with one swipe of my sword. Isn't that right, Crispin?'

'Um, so I've heard, sire,' said Crispin.

'Even so,' replied Firkin, 'I'd like to give you something to help with your quest. A magic axe perhaps that can split a rock in two? Or a hunting horn that will call the birds of the air?'

Sir Bigwart scratched his beard. 'That's very generous,' he said, 'but I'll tell you what. I don't suppose you'd be willing to part with that cooking pot of yours?'

'The pot? Of course!' said Firkin. 'Though it is quite heavy. Are you sure you can carry it?'

'Oh, don't worry – my squire will take care of that,' said Sir Bigwart.

They made their farewells and set off, promising to call in again on their way home. Crispin trudged along behind his master with the big black pot strapped to his back like a snail carrying its shell.

'Magic cooking pot!' he muttered to himself. 'A fat lot of help that's going to be!'

Chapter 8

Marigold Gets Lost

'Yikes! Is that where we're going?' gulped Crispin.

The Princess nodded. 'It's quite big, isn't it?'

'Quite big' didn't begin to describe the castle that rose out of the swirling fog ahead of them. Even from this distance it looked immense. Half-hidden in the mist, it seemed to float above Ghastly Fell like a ghostly ship. Four crumbling grey towers stood, one at each corner, their ramparts almost

touching the clouds.

Crispin shivered and drew his cloak around him. A wooden signpost pointed across the moor.

'CASTLE OF FELL – ONE MILE'

Below this someone had carved the words:

'TREZPASSERS WILL BE EATEN'

'Are you OK? Only you've gone rather pale,' said Princess Marigold.

'Me?' said Crispin. 'Just a little chilly.'

'Anyway, don't worry,' smiled Marigold. 'When we get home, you'll be able to write a poem about all this.

> *'Giants are big,*
> *Ogres are tall,*
> *Cut off their heads,*
> *And they don't bite at all.'*

She laughed, pleased with the rhyme she'd made up. Crispin had to admire her. Either she was the bravest girl he'd ever met or she didn't know much about ogres.

'Well, no point in putting it off,' said the Princess.

Sir Bigwart grabbed hold of her arm.

'Where do you think you're going?'

'To the castle, of course.'

'Are you out of your mind? We can't just walk up to the front door and knock.'

'Why not?' asked the Princess.

Why not? Marigold made it sound as if they were dropping in for tea and cake!

'There are two blood-dripping, bone-crunching ogres in that castle. They eat people. Princesses included.'

'He's right,' nodded Crispin. 'It's best to be careful.'

'What do you suggest?' asked Marigold.

'Wait a while,' advised Sir Bigwart. 'You know the saying – never slay an ogre on an empty stomach.'

'You just made that up,' said Marigold.

'No I didn't – it's in the knight's code of conduct. Anyway, I think we should set up camp here and have a spot of lunch while we work out a plan.'

'Such as?' asked the Princess.

'Well I don't know, maybe mutton broth with chicken pasties.'

'Not lunch! What sort of a *plan*?' The Princess was losing patience. Anyone would think Sir Bigwart didn't want to reach the castle at all.

'Oh, I see,' he said. 'Well, after lunch we'll keep watch to see if anyone comes out. We might need a snack just to keep us going –'

'Sir Bigwart!' the Princess interrupted.

'Yes?'

'You've never actually killed an ogre before, have you?'

'Me?' said Sir Bigwart.

'Yes. No more stories – I want the truth.'

'Well, er . . . maybe not an ogre as such,' stammered the brave knight, turning red.

'Or a giant,' said Marigold. 'Or a fire-breathing dragon. In fact you've never killed anything at all, have you?'

Sir Bigwart studied the ground sheepishly. The visor of his helmet swung down with a loud clang.

'It's true,' he admitted, pushing it back up. 'I never really wanted to come on this quest. It was my mother who pushed me into it. Up till now I've never been beyond the village.'

The Princess stamped her foot. 'You mean we've come all this way for *nothing*?' she stormed. 'It all makes sense now. No wonder you kept losing the way in the forest.'

She was marching up and down, waving her arms about. 'You never meant us to reach the castle at all, did you? Well you two brave heroes stay here if you like and discuss what you're having for lunch – I've had enough!' Saying this, she stomped off and in seconds was swallowed up by the fog.

Crispin called after her. 'Marigold! Come back! Marigold!'

Sir Bigwart shook his head. 'She's gone.'

'Gone? But you don't think she'd . . . ?'

Sir Bigwart shrugged his shoulders. 'Princesses! I told you, it's no use trying to talk to them.'

Crispin stared. Marigold was somewhere out there on Ghastly Fell, heading for the castle. They had to stop her before it was too late.

* * *

'Marigold? Marigold, where are you?'

Crispin's voice died away on the chilly air. It was hopeless. They had been trudging across the fell for what seemed like hours, but in the swirling fog it was impossible to see anything.

'Crispin!'

Crispin turned his head. The Princess's voice sounded far off and a little scared. They followed the sound until it led them to the edge of an enormous crater. The hole was a curious shape, almost as if it had been scooped out by a giant hand. At the bottom was what looked like a grubby old sheet and a very cold and muddy princess.

'Don't worry, we'll get you out,' promised Crispin. 'Wait there!'

But rescuing the Princess turned out to be harder than it looked. The hole was deep and slippery. Even when Sir Bigwart held on to Crispin's ankles and tried to lower him down, he couldn't reach the Princess's hand.

'It's no good,' groaned Sir Bigwart at last. 'We need a ladder.'

Crispin wasn't listening. The ground had started to tremble. At first it was just a small vibration, then the earth itself, the trees and the bushes actually began to shake as if an earthquake was brewing.

'What's happening?' cried Marigold. Clods of loose earth were falling in on her and she was starting to panic. Crispin gripped Sir Bigwart's arm to steady himself.

Boom – Boom – BOOM!

The ominous noise was growing louder and Crispin has a horrible feeling he knew what it was.

Boom – BOOM – BOOM!

He gasped as he glimpsed an enormous pair of muddy boots coming out of the fog. Each boot was so big he could almost have wriggled through one of the eyeholes. Above the boots a pair of legs the size of tree trunks strode along. The ogre was an astonishing sight. Crispin had never seen anyone quite as frightening in his life.

'It's them!' cried Sir Bigwart. 'Run!'

Crispin might have argued, but his master had him by the arm and dragged him behind a hawthorn bush just as Dungbean reached the hole.

From their hiding place, he saw the second ogre arrive. This one had a huge red beard falling over his belly which rose and fell like the sea. He seemed absurdly proud of this beard, stroking it constantly like a cat. Crispin saw him pick out a scrap of something and pop it into his mouth, licking his fat pink lips with relish.

'I told you,' said Grimbeard. 'I is smelling them. They is close by.'

'You is dreaming,' scoffed Dungbean. When he opened his mouth, a stomach-churning odour filled the air. Crispin thought he was going to be sick.

Grimbeard looked around. 'Whomans can be tricksy,' he muttered. 'They hide under rocks. They is close, I is telling you. I can smell their stink.'

Dungbean wiped his mouth with his sleeve. 'Well, stop your snivelling and look in the trap. I'll bet my boots 'tis empty.'

To Crispin's horror, the bearded ogre got down on his knees and peered into the hole. 'AHAAA! What is I telling you?' he cried in triumph. Thrusting in his hand, he grabbed Marigold and pulled her out.

'Got you, you little hornswoggler!' said Grimbeard. 'So who is the clever one now?'

The two ogres examined their catch. Grimbeard caught hold of Marigold's golden hair and pulled it. 'Oww!' she screamed. 'Let go of me, you brute!'

'Who is you calling a boot?' asked Grimbeard. His breath was like a warm, putrid gale. Marigold felt dizzy and wondered if she was going to faint.

She tried not to look down at the drop below or at Grimbeard's horrible mouth.

'What is a hobgoblin doing in these parts?' he asked.

'I am not a hobgoblin,' replied Marigold. 'I am the Princess Marigold.'

'A princess?' Dungbean grinned at his twin. 'I never did scoffle one of those. Does they taste sweet?'

'How should I know, you bogglehead? I never did taste one,' replied Grimbeard.

'Shall us have her roasted or frazzled in goose fat?' Grimbeard gave Marigold a poke in the ribs with his finger. ''Taint much meat on her,' he grumbled. 'She's as skinny as a goat.'

'You're right,' said Marigold. 'You wouldn't want to eat me.'

'Oh no? And why is that?'

'Princesses are all skin and bone. Look at my arms.' She rolled back the sleeves of her robe to show them her tiny wrists. Grimbeard peered at them.

"Tis true. I could snap them in half easy as a twig,' he said, scratching his thick beard thoughtfully. 'Maybe us should fatten her up.'

'Feed her bread and dripping, you mean?' said Grimbeard.

'Exactly. Then when she is plump as a porker, cook her with carrots and dumplings.'

Dungbean produced a filthy old sack and held it open.

Marigold struggled to escape. 'Let me go! Wait till my friends get here!'

Grimbeard pricked up his ears. 'Friends? What friends is you meaning?'

Marigold bit her lip. She hadn't meant to give the others away. Looking down, she caught sight of Sir Bigwart's bottom poking out from behind a bush. If the ogres caught them, there would be no one left to rescue her.

'They're on their way,' she said. 'And they're bringing an army of a hundred knights to cut off your ugly heads.'

Dungbean smiled a horrible smile. 'Let them come,' he leered. 'We will squish them like tiddly ants. And when they is dead we will cook them in a pot and throw you in to join them.'

'Meantime, enough of your jaw-twaddle,' said Grimbeard. 'In the sack you goes.'

Saying this, he dropped Marigold into his sack and the two ogres set off, striding across the foggy moor in the direction of the castle.

When the ground had stopped shaking, Sir Bigwart and Crispin crept out from behind the bush and looked at each other.

'Now we're really in trouble!' groaned Sir Bigwart.

'*We're* in trouble? What about Marigold?' asked Crispin. 'You heard them! They're going to *eat* her!'

'Right,' said Sir Bigwart. 'Which reminds me, we still haven't had any lunch.'

Chapter 9

A Very Hairy Climb

Crispin's heart was pounding as if it was trying to break out of his chest. Finding a way into the castle had been simpler than he expected. The great oak door was so huge they were both able to squirm through the gap underneath. It was more difficult for Sir Bigwart, who wasn't really designed for squirming through anything. He had insisted on bringing along Firkin's cooking pot, which made a loud clang when Crispin got it stuck under the door.

Luckily the noise went unnoticed. Crispin couldn't see what use it was going to be in any case. You could hardly threaten a hungry ogre with a cooking pot.

The room they were in seemed to be the ogres' dining hall. A fire crackled in the gigantic grate, throwing dancing shadows around the walls. Slumped in an armchair in front of it was the massive figure of Dungbean, sound asleep. His eyes were shut and his mouth lolled open. A web of dribble ran down his chin on to his leather doublet.

Crispin noticed a sour-sweet smell in the room. On the table was a gigantic pitcher containing Dungbean's home-made crab-apple cider – a drink so disgusting that no one but an ogre would have touched it. Dungbean was very proud of his secret recipe for this brew, which he made by crushing up crab apples with his bare feet. Dirt and the odd toenail turned up in the mixture but he swore this only added to the cider's powerful taste. Once he'd added salt, yeast and buckets of green water from the castle moat, he left the foaming brew to ferment for four or five years in the castle cellar.

The ogres drank the cider by the gallon, setting off belches like firecrackers and squabbling over which of them could burp the loudest and longest. When Crispin and Sir Bigwart found them, they had just finished one of these quarrels and had fallen into a deep sleep. Grimbeard had dozed off at the table, where his snores ruffled the curls of his enormous red beard. The table was bare apart from a plate of cheese crumbs and a silver birdcage as big as a church bell. Inside was Princess Marigold.

Crispin knew they didn't have much time. They had to find a way to rescue Marigold before the ogres woke up. It was impossible to climb the table legs, which were as smooth as marble pillars. There was only one way up and it would be perilous. He would have to climb Grimbeard.

Leaving the cooking pot behind, he approached the ogre's boot.

'Are you coming?' he whispered.

Sir Bigwart gazed up at the massive figure of the sleeping ogre.

'Up there? Are you out of your mind?'

'We've got to reach Marigold. I thought knights were brave.'

'They are . . . I am,' blustered Sir Bigwart. 'But one of us should stay here and keep a lookout. I mean just in case one of them wakes up.'

Crispin shrugged. If Grimbeard woke up, he thought he'd know about it soon enough. Setting his foot on the toe of the ogre's boot, he began to climb.

The first part wasn't so difficult. Back in Eggnog, Crispin had always been good at climbing trees and scaling an ogre wasn't so different. Grimbeard's filthy

trousers were riddled with holes which made good footholds. Once he reached the knobbly hills of the ogre's knees, he paused for breath. Close up, the ogre's red beard looked like a tangled forest, wild and overgrown. It hung over Grimbeard's swollen belly, rising and falling in time with his steady snores. *This is the dangerous part*, thought Crispin.

If he pulled too hard or lost his footing, the ogre would wake up – and he didn't like to think about what might happen then. Taking a deep breath, he grabbed hold of a tuft of beard and began to haul himself up.

Luckily, when Grimbeard had drunk a lot of cider he slept like a baby. But as Crispin stepped over an egg crumb, he felt the ogre shift beneath him.

''Tis mine, you snivelling weevil!' he growled. 'Give 'im here!'

Crispin hung on tight, burying his face in the ogre's horrible locks, not daring to move. Seconds passed. At last the steady rumble of Grimbeard's snoring began again. The ogre wasn't awake – he had been talking in his sleep.

Looking over his shoulder, Crispin could now see the top of the table. The gap he'd have to jump was as wide as a ditch. And if he didn't make it, the drop below was waiting. It was now or never.

Letting go, he jumped, twisting in the air and landing with a heavy thump near the table's edge. He got to his feet, relieved to see Dungbean's eyes were still closed.

'Crispin!' It was Marigold's voice. She was reaching out to him through the bars of her cage. He put a finger to his lips and went over.

'Where have you been?' she whispered impatiently. 'I've been stuck here for hours!'

Crispin sighed. 'Hello' would have been nice. Or even, 'Thanks for risking your life.'

'Stand back,' he instructed. 'I need to get the door open.'

He dragged the ogre's fork across the table and squeezed it through the bars of the cage. Using it as a lever, he pushed against it with all his weight. The catch clicked and the door sprang open with a twang. Marigold burst out and grabbed him by the hand.

'Come on!' she said. 'We have to hurry!'

'Yes, I know,' said Crispin. 'No – not that way!'

Marigold had halted at the edge of the table, staring down at the dizzying drop to the floor.

'Follow me,' said Crispin. 'We have to climb down the ogre's beard.'

But Marigold was rooted to the spot and seemed unable to move.

'It's all right,' said Crispin. 'I'll go first.'

Marigold's mouth was working and she was pointing behind him.

'R . . . ru . . . RUN!' she blurted out.

Crispin turned in time to see the shadow of a gigantic hand fall over him. He was lifted high into the air and found himself staring at the red hairs sprouting from Grimbeard's nose.

'So,' leered the ogre. 'What has we here then?'

Crispin caught sight of Marigold, who was strug-

gling to escape from Grimbeard's other hand. 'Let go of me, you big oaf!' she cried. 'Let go or I'll bite you!'

She sank her teeth into the ogre's forefinger but Grimbeard only roared with laughter.

'Call that a bite? You is weaksome as a wormwiggler!'

Grimbeard carried them over to the fireside, where he gave his brother's chair a savage kick.

'WAKE UP, YOU DOZY LUGABOUT!' he roared in Dungbean's ear.

Dungbean's eyes blinked open. He stretched up his arms and belched, filling the room with a smell like rotten apples.

'Look what I has catched!' crowed Grimbeard.

'Two?' said Dungbean, frowning. 'I swear I is only seeing one before.'

'That is 'cos I is catching another while you is sleeping like a granny,' answered Grimbeard.

'How did it get in? You think there is more of them?' asked Dungbean.

'Maybe there is,' nodded Grimbeard thoughtfully. 'Let us ask him.'

Crispin felt the ogre's grip relax and sat up on the

palm of his hand, looking into Grimbeard's blood-shot eyes. He tried not to imagine how it would feel to be crunched up like a biscuit.

'You! Hornswoggler!' growled Grimbeard. 'Is you coming alone or is you bringing with you an army?'

'I came alone,' replied Crispin, trying not to sound terrified.

'Don't listen to him! He's lying!' It was Marigold who had shouted.

Grimbeard frowned. He wasn't used to dealing with more than one opinion – it was confusing.

'He came with a knight called Sir Bigwart,' the Princess went on. 'A knight who has killed a thousand ogres bigger than you. He cuts off their heads and has them mounted on his walls. So if you don't want to die you'd better let us go before he finds you!'

As it happened, Crispin had just caught sight of the giant-killing hero in question. Sir Bigwart was stealing towards the door, dragging Firkin's cooking pot behind him.

'I is looking forward to meeting this squeak-pipping knight,' growled Grimbeard. 'I will squeeze him till his eyeballs pop and he is grizzling for mercy!'

'And I will grab him by his luglisteners and toss him into the middle of next month!' boasted Dungbean.

Crispin saw that Sir Bigwart had reached the door and was about to scramble through the narrow gap underneath. In his haste, however, he forgot that the cooking pot was a tight fit. There was a loud CLANG! as it wedged fast and wouldn't budge. The ogres heard it too and turned their heads.

'THERE'S THE LITTLE HORNSWOGGLER! CATCH HIM!' cried Grimbeard.

Chapter 10

Whoman Stew

'This is all your fault,' Marigold grumbled.

'Mine?' said Sir Bigwart. He wished the Princess would stop stomping up and down. There wasn't much room in a birdcage for stomping.

'If you hadn't come on this ridiculous quest, then we wouldn't be in this mess!'

'In the first place,' said Sir Bigwart irritably, 'I never asked to come on this quest. And in the second place, I don't remember asking you to join me. If it's anyone's fault –'

'Oh shut up, both of you!'

Sir Bigwart and Marigold stared at Crispin in surprise. They weren't used to being told to shut up by a mere kitchen boy.

'Arguing isn't going to help,' said Crispin. 'We've got to think of a plan. We're trapped in an ogre's castle and locked in a cage, so what are our choices?'

'Escape,' said Marigold.

'Or get eaten,' said Sir Bigwart gloomily.

'But how can we escape?' asked Crispin. 'The door's bolted from the outside and the ogres will be back any minute.' He could hear Dungbean thumping around in the cellar below, looking for something.

Marigold was thinking. 'You know the story of Rapunzel?' she said.

Crispin nodded. 'The girl in the tower who lets down her hair?'

'Well, if my hair was as long as hers, you could climb down it and reach the floor.'

'Yes,' said Crispin. 'We could. Except your hair doesn't reach your waist.'

'No,' said Marigold. 'I'm just saying if it was.'

This didn't seem to be getting them very far.

Crispin sat down on the upturned cooking pot, trying to think. 'If only we had something to bargain with,' he said.

'You can offer them him,' suggested Marigold, looking at Sir Bigwart.

'Or her,' replied Sir Bigwart.

Crispin gave up. They didn't have anything to bargain with. Besides the clothes they were wearing, the only thing they had was Firkin's pot. He jumped to his feet. Why hadn't he thought of it before? The ogres would certainly be interested in a magic cooking pot. They talked about little else but what they were going to eat. An idea began to take shape in Crispin's mind. It would take courage but it was better than sitting around waiting to be eaten.

Just then the door slammed and Grimbeard entered the castle carrying armfuls of wood. He had been out on Ghastly Fell pulling up trees by the roots. He snapped them in two with his bare hands and threw them on to the fire. Before long the room was lit by a crackling blaze.

Dungbean emerged from the steps of the cellar armed with a greasy collection of pots and pans. 'How shall us cook them then?' he asked. 'Shall us sizzle them in a sausage pan and guzzle them whole?'

Grimbeard wrinkled his nose. 'Last time you is doing that you is setting alight your hair. Sizzling is no good. I say us puts them in the oven and bakes them till they're crispling.'

Dungbean shook his head. 'You is talking hogswoggle! That oven isn't working since you tried to mend it with a hammer. No, if we is cooking them, boiling is best. Let us have them in a stew.'

'A stew?' repeated Grimbeard.

'Yes, you slugbucket! A whoman stew with turnips and taters and salt and pepper. There is nothing half as tasty as a hot whoman stew with the heads floating on the top.'

Princess Marigold couldn't help hearing this conversation since the ogres practically shouted every word. She turned away feeling sick. Sir Bigwart had his fingers in his ears.

As darkness fell, the ogres went about preparing the great feast they had planned for that evening. Dungbean ferried buckets of green, murky water from the castle moat and poured them into the big rust-coloured stewpot that hung over the fire.

94

His twin brother sat at the table chopping enormous turnips, potatoes and fat red onions with an
axe. The onions made his eyes run and his nose drip
on to the food but he didn't pause to wipe them.

'Is her hot and bubbling yet?' he asked every five
minutes.

'No, it isn't! You is frying my patience asking that!'
growled Dungbean.

At last Crispin saw clouds of steam start to rise
from the stewpot and heard the sound of bubbling
hot water. The moment had come.

'Now for the best part,' grinned Grimbeard crookedly. 'Shall us toss them in all at once or do them one at a time?'

Crispin felt Marigold move closer to him. Her hand crept into his and squeezed it.

'Let me go first,' he whispered. 'I've got an idea.'

'Us'll take it in turns,' Dungbean was saying. 'I likes to hear them squalling when they is boiling in the pot. Hand me the cage, slugbucket, and I will toss the first one in.'

'Not on your bellies,' growled Grimbeard. 'I made the stew so I is going first.'

'*I* is!'

'I IS!'

The cage swung around dizzily in Grimbeard's hand as the two ogres squabbled and fought over it. Dungbean stamped on his brother's foot and Grimbeard headbutted him in the belly. The three prisoners were tossed about in the cage like leaves in a gale as the ogres punched, bit, spat and cursed each other with filthy names. Finally Dungbean managed to poke his brother in the eye and steal the cage from his grasp.

He unlatched the door and pushed his hand inside.

'Come on, my beauties! Who's first for the pot?' he said.

Marigold backed away and Sir Bigwart clung to the bars of the cage.

Dungbean's hand closed around Crispin, who made no attempt to escape.

He was carried over to the fire. Hot clouds of steam rose up to sting his eyes. Below him, the lumpy, pea-green stew boiled and bubbled like lava.

'Wait!' he cried. 'I've something to tell you.'

'Save your breaths,' grinned Dungbean. 'In you goes.'

Chapter 11

A Horrible Way to Go

Crispin found himself hanging upside down by one leg and about to fall.

'Listen to me!' he gasped. 'There's something I want to show you!'

'What is he drivelling about?' asked Grimbeard, rubbing his eye. 'Toss the swiddler in.'

'It's a cooking pot,' cried Crispin, swaying back and forward. 'A MAGIC cooking pot.'

'Hogswoggle!' sneered Grimbeard. ''Tain't no such

thing. Let him go.'

He jogged his brother's arm and Crispin felt himself falling. He hurtled downwards through clouds of hot steam towards the scalding soup below. This was it – the end.

All the air was knocked out of him as he landed. Except there was no splash and no hot, bubbling stew closing over him. Instead he found himself face down on the palm of a giant hand which was lifting him up. At the last moment Dungbean must have reached out and caught him.

'Magic?' asked Dungbean. 'What is you twaddling about?'

'He is telling fibwigglers. Sling him back in!' grumbled Grimbeard.

'It's the truth!' panted Crispin. He knew this was his last chance. 'It's a magic cooking pot. I brought it to show you. If you don't believe me, look in the cage!'

Dungbean set him down on the table while he searched the birdcage.

A moment later he returned with Firkin's cooking pot, which to him was little bigger than a sugar bowl.

'This teensy thing?' he said.

'It may not look much,' said Crispin, 'but it belonged to a great and powerful wizard called Firkin of the Forest. He gave it to me.'

He glanced back at the cage. Marigold and Sir Bigwart could only watch, knowing that if Crispin's plan failed, they were next for the stew.

'What magic is you doing with such a piffling thing?' demanded Grimbeard.

'Put it on the table and I'll show you,' replied Crispin.

Dungbean did as he was told and sat down at the table opposite his brother. The promise of seeing

magic at work was too good to resist. They waited eagerly to see what Crispin had in mind.

'Have you ever tasted honey cakes?' he asked.

'Honey cakes? What is they?' replied Dungbean.

'Let me show you.'

Crispin approached the pot, remembering Firkin's warning not to get too close when it was cooking. He closed his eyes, praying that he could remember the right words.

Grimbeard and Dungbean both leaned forward, their mouths hanging open. Crispin stretched out his hands and spoke in a loud voice.

'Cooking pot, cooking pot,
Hear my request,
Bake me some honey cakes.
Make them the best.'

For a second or two nothing happened. Grimbeard scowled.

'I told you. 'Tis nothing but a swizzling trick!'

'Wait!' said Dungbean. 'Look!'

Clouds of blue-grey smoke were rising from the pot. It began to bubble and tremble. The smoke grew thicker, turning from blue to green to violet. At last the pot gave an echoing belch and out flew a plate which Crispin just managed to catch. The sweet smell of freshly baked honey cakes filled the room.

'Well I'll be frazzled!' exclaimed Dungbean.

'I never seed the like!' said Grimbeard, peering at the stack of cakes. 'Is they for scoffling?'

'Of course. Try them,' urged Crispin, holding out the plate.

Grimbeard greedily scooped up a half dozen while his twin brother snatched the plate and tipped the rest straight into his mouth.

'Scumshous!' declared Dungbean, smacking his lips.

'Yes, that has wettled my appetite nicely,' agreed Grimbeard. 'And now time you went back in the stew!' He rose from his seat and snatched Crispin from the table.

'No! Wait!' cried Crispin, struggling to escape. 'There's more!'

'More?' repeated Grimbeard. 'What more?'

'I haven't even begun. The pot can cook you any-thing you want. All you have to do is ask.'

Grimbeard frowned. '*Anything?* You mean anything we want?'

'Anything at all,' nodded Crispin.

'Put him down, bimstinkle,' ordered Dungbean.

Grimbeard glared. 'I will decide whether I is putting him down or not!'

He put Crispin down.

'Can it cook devilled kidneys?' he asked.

'And whoman brains in onion sauce?' added Dungbean. Dribble was escaping from his mouth and dripping on the table.

'It can cook you anything you want,' said Crispin. 'But there is one dish so rich and spicy, I'm afraid you wouldn't have the stomach for it.'

'US? Not have the BELLIES for it?' roared Grimbeard. 'You is talking out of your ears!'

'There is nothing I cannot eat! I is crunching up bones since I is a baby!' declared Dungbean. He smashed his fist down so close to Crispin that he had to jump back to avoid being flattened.

'That may be true,' said Crispin, holding his nerve, 'but I only ever met one person who could eat this dish and that was the Great Ogre of the North. He has it every Sunday for his lunch.'

'HA!' scoffed Grimbeard. 'Who is this gobtrotting ogre? You think he is mightsier than the great Grimbeard?'

'Bring me this dish and I will swallop it down before you can count to three!' vowed Dungbean.

'Very well,' said Crispin. 'Then ask the magic pot to bake you Ogre Pie.'

'Ogre Pie?' Dungbean frowned. 'I is never hearing of it!'

'The Ogre of the North says it's his favourite pie,' said Crispin. 'That's why they named it after him.'

'Enough of your twaddle! Give me this gob-smacking pie!' cried Dungbean, thumping the table impatiently. 'I is slathering to taste it!'

'Then speak to the pot and tell it what you want,' said Crispin.

Dungbean narrowed his eyes. 'Why must us tell it? Why doesn't you?' he asked.

'Because it will only grant one wish a day and I have already used mine,' replied Crispin. This seemed to satisfy the ogres, who were only too eager to try some magic themselves.

Crispin taught them the words of the spell. It took a bit of practice since the ogres were slow learners and kept blaming each other for muddling them up. But at long last they were ready. Dungbean took a deep breath.

'Wait,' said Crispin. 'Don't you want to see it cooking? Sit closer to the pot.'

The ogres obediently moved their chairs closer.

'Now look right into the pot and say the words I taught you.'

The ogres bent over until their noses were almost in the cooking pot. Crispin kept well back as they bellowed out the spell.

> *'COOKING POT, COOKING POT,*
> *HEAR MY REQUEST,*
> *A BIG OGRE PIE*
> *AND MAKE IT THE BEST!'*

Instantly the pot began to shake and rumble as clouds of blue smoke rose from within. The ogres bent over it excitedly.

'Tis working! I is seeing it!' cried Grimbeard.

The smoke grew thicker, changing from blue to green to violet. Suddenly there was a bolt of light accompanied by a noise like the sky splitting in two. Crispin, Marigold and Sir Bigwart turned away to shield their eyes.

When they looked again, a gigantic pie had bloomed from the pot. The crust bulged over the sides and oozed a rich, dark gravy. As for Dungbean and Grimbeard, they had vanished from sight. Nothing of them remained but two pairs of leather boots smoking on the floor.

Chapter 12

Eggnog Again

King Eggnog stared out of the palace window and sighed. It was almost a week now since his beloved Marigold had disappeared and he was beginning to wonder if he would ever see her again. Meals were eaten in the Great Hall in silence while the knights drooped around the castle, not knowing what to do with themselves.

'A search party!' said the King, turning round suddenly.

'I beg your pardon, sire?' asked Lord Fawnley, wiping his nose. He was nursing a dreadful cold.

'We should send one out, Fawnley! A search party!'

'My lord, we sent one already. The day before yesterday.'

'Did we? Why didn't you say so? What did they find?'

'I regret they – *a . . . a . . . atchoo!* – haven't returned yet,' wheezed Lord Fawnley. 'I fear they could be lost.'

'Lost? How can they be lost?'

'Don't worry, sire, I have sent a . . . a . . . another one.'

'Well?'

'Well what, my lord?'

'Did the search party searching for the search party manage to find them?'

Lord Fawnley looked embarrassed. 'No, my lord. It seems they are lost too.'

'Odds frogs! Fawnley! Marigold is missing! Anything could have happened to her.' The King was having to raise his voice because of all the noise coming from the courtyard. 'What is the use of one hundred knights . . .' he began.

'Ninety-nine knights, sire,' corrected Lord Fawn-ley. 'I fear Sir Bigwart may be . . . how shall I put it?'

'What?'

'Dead, my lord. You remember you sent him to find the Ogres of Ghastly Fell? I'm afraid he hasn't come back.' Lord Fawnley dabbed at his nose sorrowfully.

'Great heavens!' said the King. 'Bigwart as well? How long has he been gone?'

'Since Saturday, sire.'

The King looked at him. 'Saturday? Isn't that when Marigold went missing?'

'I'm a . . . a . . . afraid so. *Aatchoo!*'

'Odds frogs! You don't think she went with him?'

Lord Fawnley's answer was drowned out by the commotion outside the window. A crowd was cheer-ing wildly and drums and trumpets could be heard coming up the hill from the village. King Egg-nog went to the window to see what on earth was happening.

Through the castle gates came a farm cart sur-rounded by an excited crowd. Seated at the front was Sir Bigwart holding the reins. With him was his squire, Crispin, the Wizard Firkin dressed in his best hat, and Princess Marigold herself, looking as if she'd just returned from her holidays. King Eggnog was so overjoyed that he rushed downstairs to meet them, forgetting he was wearing his slippers.

That night a banquet was held in the Great Hall. The returning hero, Sir Bigwart, was the guest of honour. Princess Marigold sat on the King's right and Firkin on his left. King Eggnog had never met a real wizard before and was keen to see what he could do. Crispin didn't sit at the table at all, since he was only a humble squire and belonged with the servants.

King Eggnog got to his feet and waited for the room to fall quiet.

'Let us raise our goblets,' he said, 'to the bold Sir Bigwart who killed the Ogres of Ghastly Fell and brought the Princess Marigold safely back.'

'To the brave Sir Bigwart!' chorused the knights of Eggnog, rising to their feet.

Lord Fawnley leaned across and whispered something in the King's ear.

'Good heavens, I almost forgot!' said the King. 'Next Saturday you are all invited to the Princess Marigold's wedding.'

'WEDDING?' Marigold jumped to her feet and reached for a bowl of soup. King Eggnog prepared to duck.

'But surely, my sweet . . . the quest? We agreed . . .'

The Princess pointed at Sir Bigwart. 'If you think that I'm going to marry that knightly nincompoop you can think again!'

Lord Fawnley blew his nose. 'I'm afraid, Highness, the King gave his word. Sir Bigwart completed the quest so you must – *Aatchoo!* – marry him.'

'But what if he didn't complete the quest?' said Marigold.

'Well, of course he did! Didn't you, Sir Bigwart?' asked the King.

Sir Bigwart had turned a little pink and was suddenly interested in his supper.

'Well . . . ah um . . .' he mumbled.

'Did you slay the ogres or did you not?' demanded Lord Fawnley.

'Well, I um . . . I . . . not,' admitted Sir Bigwart in a small voice.

'Odds frogs, man!' cried the King. 'If you didn't then who in heaven's name did?'

A small boy with a pudding bowl haircut pushed his way through the crowds until he was standing in front of the King. He bowed clumsily.

'YOU?' said King Eggnog. 'Who are you?'

'This is Crispin, Father,' smiled Marigold. 'He's a squire and he makes the best honey cakes you've ever tasted.'

'And he killed the ogres?' asked the King.

Crispin bowed again. He seemed to have lost his tongue.

'And saved your life?'

'He did, Father,' smiled the Princess. Crispin bowed a third time.

'Well then, I suppose now you wish to marry my daughter?'

'He doesn't,' answered Marigold before Crispin could open his mouth. 'He wants to be a knight. And he's going to live at the palace. Isn't that right, Crispin?'

'Um, yes, I suppose it is,' said Crispin and blushed to his boots because the Princess had just kissed him on the cheek, which is enough to make the bravest of knights turn red.

Lord Fawnley leaned across to address the King. 'Well, sire, it all seems to have turned out for the best,' he said. 'Sir Bigwart is back, the ogres are dead and the Princess seems to have – *Aatchoo!* – found a friend.'

'Yes,' said King Eggnog, wiping his eye. 'But I do wish you'd stop sneezing all over me.'

The Wizard Firkin spoke up. 'If you will allow me,

my lord,' he said, 'I know just the spell for curing a cold.'

He drew out his wand and waved it twice over Fawnley's head, uttering some strange words. Instantly the Lord Chamberlain vanished in a puff of blue smoke. In his place stood a hairy hog which blinked in surprise, opened its mouth – and sneezed.

Sir Bigwart smiled to himself. He had always said that Lord Fawnley was a terrible boar.